QUICKLY'S MAGICAL PANCAKE ADVENTURE

Dear Phyllis...

Award Winning Team:

Miriam Kronish & Jeryl Abelmann

Illustrations by **Chason Matthams**

Happy Pancaking...

Love

Jeryl

Quickly's Magical Pancake Adventure
First Edition Hardcover copyright © 2013

Summary: Quickly, The Magic Spatula, searches for the best pancake recipes he can find, blending a magical adventure with a treasure trove of delicious pancake recipes.

Visit us on the web!
www.QuicklyTheMagicSpatula.com | www.QuicklysMagicalPancakeAdventure.com

ISBN 978-1-60746-550-8 Paperback
ISBN 978-1-60746-107-4 Hardcover
ISBN 978-1-60746-022-0 ebook

Printed in the United States of America by Bookmasters
30 Amberwood Parkway
Ashland, Ohio 44805
January 2013, D11426

Published by Wavecrest
3131 Bascom Ave. Suite 150
Campbell, CA 95008
wavecrest.fastpencil.com

Dedicated to chefs everywhere …

who constantly strive to please people's palates

CHAPTER ONE

Hello, readers! My name is Quickly, The Magic Spatula. Here I am in a frame on the kitchen wall, where I've lived, beloved by my family, for many years.

You might wonder how I got my name in the first place.

Well, a long time ago, I used to help make the pancakes every Sunday morning in Mommy's kitchen. Mommy made the best pancakes in the world and people came from far and wide to eat at her table.

When they asked her what was the secret of her delicious pancakes, she always said it was me, her trusty spatula. She said she just couldn't make them without me.

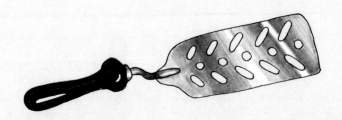

One day, she was all ready to flip the first batch of her Silver Dollar Pancakes, when she realized that she'd forgotten to get me. "Jeffrey! Jeffrey!" she called out to her 4-year-old son. "Please get me the spatula ... quickly!"

Little Jeffrey ran across the kitchen, found me, and ran back to Mommy. As he ran, he yelled, "Here Mommy, here's Quickly!" because he figured Quickly was my name.

And from then on, it was!

3

4

Now that you know how I got my name, I'll tell you how I got into this frame.

Every Sunday morning for years and years, Mommy and I made pancakes for the family and guests. As time went by, my paint began to peel and my luster dimmed, but I still worked my magic every time.

Eventually, the children grew up and moved away. One day, I was packed into a box with some other old kitchen favorites — and forgotten.

Then one very happy day many years later, grown-up Jeffrey and his sister were looking through boxes in the attic. They got to mine — and there I was! They were so thrilled to see me that they decided to make sure I was never out of sight again, so they placed me in a frame and let me decorate their kitchen wall.

They even gave me a special plaque with my name on it:

"*Quickly*"!

When people come to the kitchen and admire me — and they often do — it fills my heart with joy. So I've stayed in the kitchen happily for many a year.

CHAPTER TWO

Still, every once in awhile, even spatulas feel the urge
to stretch their handles a little and see the world.
For a long time, happy as I was, I dreamed of traveling —
experiencing new sights and new smells and new tastes.

Then one day it happened!

Suddenly, as I wiggled and wiggled,
I was able to slyly slide right out of
the frame. I was free!

I quickly jotted a note to my family and out the window I flew.

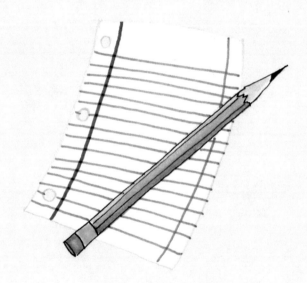

As I wondered and wandered out in the world, visions
of pancakes percolated through my mind.

"I want to learn how to make all kinds of pancakes,"
I thought. "Maybe if I meet some other spatulas …"

CHAPTER THREE

And just at that moment, a very friendly looking fellow spatula popped up by my side.

"Hello, I'm Backburner, the pancake turner. You can call me Bernie," he said. And then, as if answering my dreams, he asked, "What kinds of pancakes would you like to make?"

I told him I wanted to make as many different kinds as possible.

"Well, he replied, "I have friends from all over the world."

And thus began our great adventure in search of the world's best pancakes.

We had a lot of traveling to do, and as we set out, Bernie asked me what I knew about pancake history. I told him I didn't know much, but I'd love to find out more.

So he began to tell me a great story ...
which made the time go by quickly!

"Back in ancient times," he said, "people used to have to cook their food on fires. Pancakes started out as flatbreads baked on stones that got really hot in the flames. Think of a cake in a pan. That's what the name means: pan cake. It's a quick treat and it doesn't take as long to make as a baked cake. That's what's so great; you can make it in a pan, as fast as you can."

When he told me this, I began to grin. "Hey, *Quickly's* my name," I said, "and it means as fast as you can. I'm so very proud of my name!"

"There is a recipe for pancakes in *Apicius*, an ancient Roman cookbook," Bernie went on. "But those pancakes were served differently than we serve them now. People ate them with pepper and honey."

I asked him how pancakes first came to America — and Bernie knew that story, too.

"The English and Dutch settlers brought their recipes with them to the colonies when they came by boat to the New World," he said.

"Wow!" I said. "What a fount of knowledge you are! You seem to know everything! How come you know so much about pancakes?"

Bernie grinned proudly and bowed a little. "I am a pancake historian, Quickly," he told me. "I am always looking for new facts about pancakes. And now it's so much more fun to look, with a good friend like you to keep me company!"

CHAPTER
FOUR

We were strolling along, open to whatever came our way, when we suddenly noticed a large billboard by the side of the road. On it was a picture of a huge, scrumptious looking stack of pancakes and the words:

INTERNATIONAL SPATULA CAMP!
Calling All Spatulas!

What could be batter — I mean better — than this timely gathering of spatulas from around the world? The only word I could think of for this fortuitous bit of knowledge was … serendipity.

Now it was Bernie's turn to ask a question.
"What does that mean?" Bernie queried.

"Serendipity means coming upon something by chance in a very happy way," I told him, smiling my biggest smile in anticipation of what was to come.

It seemed as if this camp had been set up with us in mind.

I had never gone to camp before and neither had Bernie. We raced to the campgrounds in the center of town. And as we approached the doors to the main building, we saw spatulas of every shape and kind, chatting with excitement as they walked in.

What a scene! There were metal spatulas and wooden ones, shiny ones and colorful ones, some with round holes and some with narrow slits, and old ones with their luster worn down by long experience. A few were very tall with no slits at all; others were short and squat.

How fortunate we were to find ourselves in such a diverse family!

As we walked in the door, a shiny spatula greeted us and handed us a fat booklet full of camp activities.

What should we do? Where should we go first? There were so many tantalizing choices!

We could watch famous chefs make pancakes, listen to pancake stories, swap pancake recipes, write pancake poems, and sing pancake songs.

Or we could just take it all in, strolling through the Grand Exhibition Hall full of everything pancake.

All around us we saw pancake pans and pancake griddles, chefs' implements and chefs' clothing, and recipe books and brochures for pancake restaurants.

There was everything — even a booth featuring pancake make-up!

CHAPTER FIVE

We were wandering around, bedazzled by the many choices before us, when suddenly we heard a chorus! On the stage in the Exhibition Hall, a large group of spatulas were singing lustily. Their song was *In Praise of Pancakes*, to the tune of *You Are My Sunshine*. Want to try your hand at singing it? Here are the words:

We are the chorus
And we are with you
We're here to welcome one and all
We know that you'll learn
So much together
That you'll say,
"We had a ball!"

Pancakes are perfect
When they are sizzling
Upon your griddles
Large and small
Just turn them over
And then you serve them
Throughout the world
To one and all.

So check your booklets
And choose the sessions
That are most tempting to your moods
We know that **you** are
The reason pancakes
Are among folk's favorite foods!

We clapped and cheered when their song was over and they took their bows and walked off the stage.

There were so many things to do that Bernie and I decided to split up. That way we could cover more ground.

We promised to meet in the cafeteria when the sessions were over. But we could barely sit still, we were both so excited to start our sessions, to meet spatulas from all over and learn more pancake facts.

Spatulas from everywhere crowded into the different rooms. Just imagine the scene — all of us so fidgety and excited that we couldn't help flipping over with joy.

I chose the session on

Pancake Tips

And the presenter had so many, I never stopped scribbling. Here's what I managed to write down:

Pancake Tips for Spatulas who are Beginners:

- Be sure to read your recipe all the way through before starting.

- Assemble all your necessary tools and ingredients: measuring spoons, measuring cups, bowls for batter, wooden spoons, flour, eggs, milk, and anything else you need.

- A cast-iron pan, a griddle, or a nonstick skillet work best.

- Set your griddle or pan to medium heat.

- As you prepare the batter, mix the dry ingredients in one bowl and the wet ingredients in another and then mix them together.

- If you separate your eggs, the pancakes will be fluffier. Add just the yolks first and wait until the last step in the process before adding the well-beaten whites of the eggs to the batter.

- After you have prepared the batter, wait for five to fifteen minutes before cooking.

- Your first pancake will tell you if the pan is heated to the right temperature.

- The first pancake is usually not the best of the batch — don't worry, the rest will be fine.

- An ice cream scoop is an excellent kitchen utensil to scoop the batter.

- When you see the bubbles forming on the top and browning a little around the edges, it's time to flip the pancakes.

- Serve the pancakes right away if you can — but if you have to wait, place the pancakes in a warm oven at 200°F.

Although my pancakes were always superb, it was heartwarming for me to hear these tips. The presenter reinforced my confidence in pancake making.

CHAPTER
SIX

Bernie went to a session called *All the World Loves Pancakes*, and when we met up again, he couldn't wait to tell me everything.

He was clutching a long list of *The ABCs of Pancakes* from far and wide.

"Wow!" he said grinning. "Even I had no idea there were so many kinds of pancakes out there. I can't wait to make some of them!"

As we munched on a yummy lunch of pancakes called dorayaki — which are pancakes from Japan — Bernie shared his pancake list with me.

ABCs of PANCAKES

A
apom balik.....Malaysia, Singapore
ataif.............................Middle East

B
baghrir.............................Morocco
ban chian kuih.....................China
bao bing...........................China
bin-jatuk..........................Korea
black-eyed bean....................Africa
blini.............................Russia
blintz.....................Eastern Europe
buckwheat..........................U.S.
buttercake.........................U.S.

C
cannelloni.........................Italy
chapatti...........................India
chataamari.........................Nepal
corncake...........................U.S.
crêpe............................France
creier de ritel pane...........Romania
cripf............................England
crumpet..........................Scotland

D
dadar gutung....................Indonesia
drop-scone......................Scotland
dorayaki.........................Japan
dosa.............................India

E
eterkuckas.........................France
(Alsace Lorraine region)
eierkuchen........................Germany

F
farinata...........................Italy
flaeskpannkaka....................Sweden
flannel cake.......................U.S.
flapjack....................U.S., Canada
flat car...........................U.S.
flapper...........................U.S.
flensje...................the Netherlands
frayse...........European Middle Ages

G
galette...........................France
griddlecake................U.S., Canada

H
hoecake....................U.S., Canada
hotcake...........................U.S.

I
injera...........................Ethiopia

J
jeon.............................Korea
johnnycake.........................U.S.

K
kartoffelpuffer...................Germany

L
latke ....Eastern Europe
lefse ....Norway

M
moo shu..........................China

N
nalesniki..........................Poland

O oatmeal.....................................U.S.
okonomiyaki...........................Japan

P palacsinta............................Hungary
palatschinken.........................Austria
pannekoeke.................South Africa
pannekoeken.....the Netherlands
pannukahu...............................Finland
pfannkuchen......................Germany
pikelets....England, New Zealand,
Australia
plåttar..................................Sweden
ployes.....................French Canadian
poffertje.................the Netherlands
poh pia..............................Singapore
po-ping...................................China

Q qata-ef.......................Egypt, Syria

R raggmunk.......Norway, Denmark,
Sweden
rårakor..............Norway, Sweden,
Denmark
reibekuchen.......................Germany
rice cake.........Nepal, Philippines
round-robin..............................U.S.
roti.....................................Thailand
rova dosa...............................India

S scallion..................................China
slapjack....................................U.S.
socca....................................France

T tiganites..............................Greece
tortilla.....Mexico, Latin America

U Ulster..................................Scotland

V vegan.......................................U.S.
Vermont....................................U.S.

W wheat-flour........the Netherlands
wein palalschinken.........Austria

X xèo xèo...............................Vietnam

Y Yorkshire pudding........England

Z zucchini....................................U.S.

35

With my head swimming with so many exotic pancake names, I wanted nothing more than to taste them. "Wouldn't it be great," I said to Bernie, "if we could visit all the chefs in the world and see how they make them?"

"Sure," Bernie said. "But what's so great is we don't have to. There's a session called *Great Chefs' Pancakes* starting right now!"

"Yippee!" I yelled, and away we went — licking our lips in anticipation.

The room was overflowing with spatulas — this session was not to be missed. Extra chairs were added and a parade of great chefs sauntered onto the stage, smiling broadly.

Each chef proudly shared a special recipe. We all cheered as they took their turns.

Bernie and I collected all the new recipes and placed them in our backpacks.

"These sweet and savory pancakes will be a welcome addition to my family's kitchen," I said to all the spatulas who joined us afterwards at a cafeteria table.

"We'd like to know what you learned today," I asked them all. "The more we learn from each other, the more each one of us will know."

The tales unfolded as the afternoon lengthened into early evening. Each spatula had a tale to tell.

"I learned about Pancake Day," said a tall, tawny spatula named PanDora.

"What's Pancake Day?" everyone asked her at once.

PanDora explained that a long time ago, in the United Kingdom, Pancake Day was held the Tuesday before the Lenten season begins. This special day has many names — Pancake Day, Pancake Tuesday, and Shrove Tuesday. On Pancake Day it was the custom to eat pancakes — stack after stack of them!

A little boy sitting next to Bernie spoke up excitedly. He stood out because he was a boy, not one of us.

"Hi," he said. "I'm Henry, a direct descendant of British settlers who brought our family's first spatula to these shores so long ago. When I first heard about the Spatula Camp I couldn't wait to come here and meet all of you — and here I am!"

Everyone smiled at Henry and welcomed him into the group.

CHAPTER SEVEN

As we sat together and listened to each other's tales, I thought about how much we spatulas have in common. We all enrich our families' lives. And we're all proud to do so.

Even though we hail from different parts of the world, with different languages and different customs, we all have the same goals: to do our jobs as well as we can, to excite our eaters' taste buds, and make breakfast time — or any pancake time — one of joy and hope and peace.

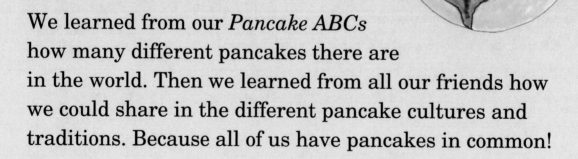

We learned from our *Pancake ABCs* how many different pancakes there are in the world. Then we learned from all our friends how we could share in the different pancake cultures and traditions. Because all of us have pancakes in common!

Wouldn't it be wonderful if, instead of fighting, the peoples of the world could live together as one big happy pancake-eating family ...

just like we are doing at Spatula Camp?

44

As our camp drew to a close I looked through my notes
and hastily scribbled a poem.

~ A Pancake Poem ~

Pancakes, pancakes, by the score

Some are sweet and some are savory

You can make each one with bravery

And they all have so much flavory

That your mouth will beg for more

Pancakes, pancakes, by the score!

And when you want to have some more,

You just have to yell, "Encore!"

With a smile and a wave, I bid a
fond farewell to all my new friends
and gave each of them a copy of my
pancake poem as a good-bye present.

And now, it's time for me to return to my own family …
and to my special place on the wall.

In less time than it takes to say …

Quickly: The Magic Spatula

… here I am *at home* where I belong.

My thoughts happily return again and again to my
Magical Pancake Adventure and all the recipes I
collected from the *Great Chefs' Session.*

I am so excited to share these pancake recipes with
you — and I hope you'll share them with your friends
and your family.

My final tip:

Cooking can be tricky.
Why not ask a parent or a friend to give you a hand?
Until my next adventure …

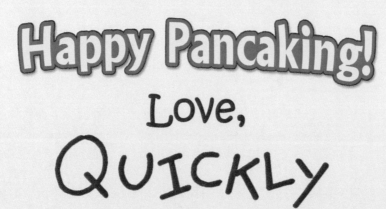

Happy Pancaking!
Love,
QUICKLY

QUICKLY'S RECIPE COLLECTION

Chef Quickly

Gold Medal Winner | *Quickly: The Magic Spatula*

MOMMY'S SILVER DOLLAR PANCAKES

Ingredients:

1 cup sour cream
1 cup cottage cheese
1 tablespoon maple syrup
½ teaspoon pure vanilla extract
4 large eggs, separated
1 tablespoon sugar
¾ cup flour
unsalted butter, for greasing the griddle

Preparation:

Combine sour cream, cottage cheese, maple syrup, vanilla extract, and egg yolks.

Beat thoroughly.

Slowly add flour to batter and continue to stir.

Add sugar to egg whites and beat until stiff. Fold into batter.

Lightly butter a griddle.

Ladle about 3 tablespoons of the batter for each silver dollar pancake.

Cook until the bottom side is nicely browned.

Turn pancake over and cook on the other side until browned.

Continue ladling the batter and cooking the pancakes until all the batter is used. Stir the batter from the bottom as the bottom is used to maintain the consistency.

If desired, add fruit to the batter, such as blueberries, strawberries, raspberries, banana slices, or a combination of fruit.

Serve them "quickly" with warmed maple syrup!

Serves 4 – 6

Chef Jacques Pépin

POTATO CRÊPES WITH CAVIAR

Ingredients for the Crêpes:

1 large potato (about 9 ounces)
2 tablespoons all-purpose flour
2 large whole eggs
1 additional egg white
⅓ cup milk
¼ teaspoon salt
⅛ teaspoon hot pepper sauce
4 tablespoons canola oil

For the Crêpes:

Put the potato in a saucepan with water to cover, and bring to a boil.

Cover, reduce the heat, and boil gently for 45 minutes, until the potato is tender.

Drain, peel, and press the potato through a food mill into a bowl.

Add the flour, whole eggs, and egg white, and mix well with a whisk.

Then mix in the milk, salt, and hot pepper sauce.

In a skillet, heat 2 teaspoons of the oil.

When hot, add about ¼ cup of the crêpe mixture, which should spread to create a circle 4½ to 5 inches in diameter.

Cook over medium heat for about 2 minutes on each side.

Transfer to a cookie sheet, and set aside in a warm oven while you make 3 more crêpes with the remaining batter and oil.

continued ...

Chef Jacques Pépin
POTATO CRÊPES WITH CAVIAR

Ingredients for Garnishes:

about 8 ounces natural red salmon caviar (about 12 tablespoons)
about 1 cup sour cream
1 tablespoon finely chopped fresh chives
3 tablespoons (about 2 ounces) beluga, osetra, or sevruga caviar,
    preferably *malossol* (lightly salted)

For the Garnishes:

To serve, spread the entire top surface of the lukewarm crêpes with red caviar
(about 2 tablespoons on each), extending the caviar clear to the edge of each crêpe.

Mound 2 rounded tablespoons of sour cream in the center
of each crêpe and sprinkle with the chives.

Finally, spoon about 1½ teaspoons of black caviar
in the center of each sour cream mound.

Serve immediately.

*"The classic way of serving caviar is with buckwheat pancakes and frozen
vodka. It is an expensive treat and serving it with potato crêpes is quite special
and less expensive. These crêpes, made from a batter that contains just two
whole eggs, are served covered with red caviar, the amount adjusted to suit your
pocketbook. Then to make the dish superlative, I use a little of the expensive
black caviar from sturgeon — beluga, osetra, or sevruga — as a garnish."*

Serves 4

Chef Francesca Thorn

International Personal Chef – Land & Sea | Private International Yacht Chef
The Caribbean & Mediterranean

CARIBBEAN CITRUS CRAB CRÊPES

Ingredients:

1 cup whole milk
¼ cup half & half
4 eggs
2 tablespoons melted butter
1 lemon, zested
¾ cup flour
2 tablespoons sugar
1 good pinch of salt

Filling:

16 ounces of your favorite crabmeat
4 ounces cream cheese
1 teaspoon lemon juice
1 head of bib lettuce
1 bunch of asparagus, blanched
    (use the top 6 inches only)
8 ounces chopped pineapple, drained
1 scallion, chopped
    (use the green part only)
¼ cup chopped macadamia nuts

Dressing:

Combine and Shake:
½ cup coconut oil
¼ cup light olive oil
½ cup raspberry vinegar
2 tablespoons orange juice
1 teaspoon lemon juice
½ teaspoon celery salt
1 teaspoon honey

Crêpe Preparation:

Using a wire whisk, combine the milk, half & half, and eggs. Set aside.

Combine melted butter and lemon zest. Set aside.

Combine flour, sugar, and salt.

Slowly add flour mixture into the milk mixture.

Whisk for 1 minute until everything is mixed and the batter is smooth.

Add melted butter mixture and whisk about 20 strokes.

Hint: The key for a good-looking crêpe is to be sure the skillet is hot!

Chef Francesca Thorn

CARIBBEAN CITRUS CRAB CRÊPES

Crêpe Preparation *(continued)*:

Pre-heat a skillet with a little butter. When the butter begins to sizzle, pour about 3 tablespoons batter into skillet.

Hint: The process goes *quickly* ... so have the spatula ready!

Cook the crêpe about 25 seconds until the top begins to dry, then flip the crêpe and cook about 10 seconds and remove. *Phew!* Repeat the process until all the batter is gone. The crêpes can be stacked and frozen if you don't use them all.

Building Your Caribbean Citrus Crêpe:

Make sure ALL ingredients are chilled.
The dressing is best at room temperature.

Combine crab, cream cheese, and lemon.
Mix until combined. Salt to taste.

Take one crêpe and layer it with a leaf of bib lettuce, 3 asparagus, 2 tablespoons crab mixture, 1 tablespoon pineapple, a sprinkle of scallion, and a sprinkle of nuts. Wrap, fold, or roll, and drizzle with dressing!

"This recipe was made with fresh conch before it was ever made with crab. Conch didn't run, pinch, or hide. It was prepared with fresh papaya and served with a spicy citrus dressing made from roasted Chilean peppers. Also, blanched broccoli or thin slices of cucumber work as a nice substitute for the asparagus."

Serves 8

Chef Charles Phan

Executive Chef & Owner | The Slanted Door | The Ferry Building
San Francisco, California

BÁNH XÈO
VIETNAMESE CRÊPE WITH PORK, SHRIMP, AND FLAVORED FISH SAUCE

Ingredients for Batter:

1 cup rice flour, packed
½ cup cornstarch, packed
¼ teaspoon turmeric powder
¼ cup coconut milk
2 cups water
½ teaspoon salt
½ cup green onions, chopped ¼ inch thick
¼ cup dried mung bean, peeled and split (optional)
2 – 4 tablespoons of water   (if using dried mung bean)

Ingredients for Filling:

¾ cups neutral oil (canola, grape seed, or corn)
½ pound lean pork shoulder or butt, slice into
    1 inch x 2 inch pieces, about ⅛ inch thick
1 small yellow onion,
    peeled and sliced ¼ inch thick
6 cups mung bean sprouts
15 medium shrimp, cleaned and sliced
    in half lengthwise
24 leaves of lettuce (for serving, 4 per crêpe)
6 sprigs of mint (for serving, 1 per crêpe)

Ingredients for Nuoc Nam (Flavored Fish Sauce):

⅓ cup fish sauce
½ cup water
½ cup white vinegar
1 tablespoon fresh lemon juice
⅓ cup granulated sugar
2 cloves garlic, minced
1 – 2 Thai chilies, minced

Preparation for Crêpes:

Soak mung bean in water for 30 minutes or overnight. Drain mung beans and puree in blender with 2 – 4 tablespoons of water until liquefied.

Combine rice flour, cornstarch, turmeric powder, coconut milk, water, salt, green onion, and mung bean. Mix well with a whisk. Let it sit for at least 10 minutes. While you are waiting, prepare other ingredients.

Note: You can prepare the batter up to 24 hours in advance.   *continued ...*

Chef Charles Phan

BÁNH XÈO
VIETNAMESE CRÊPE WITH PORK, SHRIMP, AND FLAVORED FISH SAUCE

Preparation for Crêpes *(continued)* :

Heat a 10 inch non-stick frying pan to high heat.
Add 1 teaspoon of oil.
When the oil is hot, place 4 strips of pork in the pan.
Cook until golden brown and flip to brown the other side.
Add 4 – 6 slivers of yellow onion. Cook the onion for about 30 seconds.

Stir batter. Add about ½ cup of batter to pan, lift the pan, and gently swirl the batter enough to coat the entire pan, including half way up the side of the frying pan. Keep swirling the batter until it dries out.

Place ½ – 1 cup bean sprouts and 4 pieces of shrimp on one half of the crêpe. Cover the pan. Turn heat down to medium-high and cook until the edge of the crêpe pulls away from the pan. This will take about 1 minute.

At this time, drizzle about 1 – 2 teaspoons of oil in the pan and underneath the crêpe. Try not to get the oil on top of the crêpe or it may get too greasy.

Cover the pan again and cook until shrimp is cooked through, about 1 minute. Remove lid and cook uncovered until the crêpe is crispy and golden brown on the outside. This will take about 3 – 5 minutes.

Carefully fold the empty half of the crêpe onto the half with the filling.
Use a plastic or rubber spatula. Gently remove the crêpe from the pan.
Repeat process for each additional crêpe. Stir batter each time before use.

Serve each crepe with 4 leaves of lettuce, 1 sprig of mint, and 2 ounces of the nuoc nam fish sauce. Enjoy immediately.

Use the fish sauce as a dipping sauce.
To assemble, place a piece of crêpe onto the lettuce, along with two mint leaves, and roll up the lettuce. Dip into the flavored fish sauce.

Preparation for Nuoc Nam (Flavored Fish Sauce):

Mix together fish sauce, water, vinegar, lemon juice, and sugar until sugar is dissolved. Stir in garlic and chilies right before use. Cook approximately 8 minutes per crêpe.

Makes 6 crêpes

Chef Boba Blazic
Belgrade, Serbia
BOBA'S SERBIAN CRÊPES

Ingredients for Batter:

2 eggs, separated
½ teaspoon granulated sugar
½ cup milk
⅔ cup water
½ teaspoon vanilla flavored sugar (or ¼ teaspoon vanilla extract)
1 orange, zested
1⅓ cups flour (use a bit more or less to keep batter fluid)
2 tablespoons safflower oil (or vegetable oil)

Ingredients for Filling:

⅔ cup ricotta cheese
⅓ cup small curd cottage cheese
1½ tablespoons granulated sugar

Preparation:

Mix the egg whites, granulated sugar, and milk; then the water and egg yolks; then the vanilla sugar and orange zest. Add flour and oil. Keep the batter fluid.

Cover bottom of a (12-inch) frying pan with a very small amount of oil. Pour a small amount of batter in the pan to thinly coat pan. Cook quickly on both sides.

Mix the filling ingredients, fill the crêpes, fold in half or in triangles, and serve.

"The crêpes are best when served with cold apple juice for the little ones and spiked apple cider for the adults. Pancakes in Serbia are thin, what you would call crêpes in the United States. The cheese filling is traditionally made with sremski sir, a non-salted cottage cheese from the Srem region of Serbia. This recipe was passed down to me by my grandmother, and now I enjoy preparing it often for my grandson, Marko, who adores it."

Serves 8

Chef Tracy Griffith

Sushi Chef | Author: *Sushi American Style*

APPLE-CHEDDAR DUTCH PANCAKES

Ingredients:

4 eggs
4 cups milk
a pinch of coarse salt
4½ cups all-purpose flour
1½ cups grated cheddar cheese
4 apples, peeled, cored, and thinly sliced into rings
¼ cup sugar
butter, for cooking
crème fraîche, for serving

Preparation:

Whisk eggs until slightly foamy. Add milk, whisking constantly, until combined. Add a pinch of salt, then slowly add flour, whisking or beating with a handheld electric mixer until batter is almost completely smooth.

Heat a 10 to 12 inch nonstick pan over medium-high heat.
Add about 1 teaspoon butter and swirl to coat bottom of pan.
Add about ¼ to ⅓ cup batter and tilt the pan to swirl the batter around the bottom. You may need to add a bit more to make them thicker depending on how thick the batter turns out and the size of the pan.

Sprinkle about 2 tablespoons cheddar on top.
Add apple rings (about ⅓ apple per pancake). Sprinkle with 1 teaspoon sugar.
Cook on one side until browned in spots, about 3 minutes.

Spoon about 2 tablespoons to ¼ cup batter over filling, then gently flip pancake.

The pancake may be misshapen on the first try; simply reshape — it's a very forgiving recipe. Lower heat to medium, and cook until the filling and pancake are browned, about 4 or 5 minutes more. Remove to a plate and cover. Repeat.

Serve with crème fraîche on the side.

Makes 1 dozen pancakes

Chef J. Jason O'Kennedy

Executive Chef | Hap's Original | Pleasanton, California

BANANA BLUEBERRY PANCAKES

Ingredients:

1½ cup flour
1½ teaspoons baking powder
1 teaspoon salt
1½ cups buttermilk
3 tablespoons melted butter
2 eggs
2 bananas, sliced
1 basket of blueberries

Preparation:

Mix dry ingredients together thoroughly.

Slowly mix in each of the wet ingredients, one at a time, until well incorporated.

Pour two ounces of pancake mix into a hot cast iron skillet.

Make sure that the skillet is well oiled or the bananas will stick to the skillet.

While the pancake is browning on the first side,
add sliced bananas and blueberries to the uncooked side.

Flip pancakes over once the initial side is brown and brown the other side.

Add sliced bananas and blueberries to serve.

*"Reading **Quickly** was fun for my son and me. The story was very endearing, and took me back to my childhood. It brought back memories of family breakfast every Saturday and Sunday morning with my family."*

Makes about one dozen pancakes

Chef Juvencio V. Cuellar III

6A Cafe | East Sandwich | Cape Cod, Massachusetts

BANANA BUTTERSCOTCH PANCAKES

Ingredients for Batter:

1½ bananas, plus 2 bananas for garnish
1½ cups flour
2½ teaspoons baking powder
1 cup milk
4 large eggs
4 tablespoons unsalted butter
2 tablespoons brown sugar
½ tablespoon cinnamon
2 tablespoons butterscotch topping
½ teaspoon vanilla extract

Ingredients for Sauce:

1 cup butterscotch topping
2 tablespoons butter
1 tablespoon lemon juice

Preparation for Batter:

Mash 1½ bananas and add to all other batter ingredients in a mixing bowl. Mix well until smooth.

Heat greased griddle over moderate heat. Ladle 1/4 cup batter onto griddle. Cook for 2 minutes or until little bubbles start to form.

Turn pancake over and cook on the other side for about 2 minutes.

Preparation for Sauce:

Melt butter in saucepan. Add butterscotch topping and brown sugar. Stir until the mixture is smooth. Garnish pancakes with banana slices. Pour sauce over pancakes.

Makes 8 pancakes

Chef Jeffrey Applebaum

Personal Chef | Miami, Florida

BANANA NUT PANCAKES

Ingredients:

1½ cups all-purpose flour
3½ teaspoons baking powder
1 tablespoon white sugar
1 teaspoon salt
pinch white pepper
1¼ cup milk
2 eggs
1 teaspoon almond extract
3 tablespoons butter, melted
4 bananas - 2 mashed and 2 sliced in circles
½ cup unsalted mixed nuts, chopped well

Preparation:

Preheat griddle or pan on medium heat.

Sift flour, baking powder, sugar, salt, and pepper into a large mixing bowl.

In another bowl, add milk, eggs, and almond extract.
Whisk together.

Pour wet ingredients into dry ingredients and whisk until almost smooth.

Add in melted butter, mashed bananas, and chopped nuts.

Mix until smooth without over mixing batter.

Lightly oil pan and spoon batter in evenly.

Arrange sliced bananas into the wet batter while cooking.

Brown evenly and flip over to finish.

Serves 8 – 10

Chef Antonio J. Cardoso

Executive Sous Chef | Courtesy of The Ritz-Carlton New York, Central Park

BUTTERMILK PANCAKES WITH CARAMELIZED BANANAS

Ingredients:

1 cup all-purpose flour
1 teaspoon baking soda
½ teaspoon salt
1 large egg, lightly beaten
1 lemon, zested
1 cup well-shaken buttermilk
vegetable oil, for brushing griddle
½ cup white granulated sugar
2 bananas
confectioner's sugar
2 strawberries, sliced in half

Preparation:

Whisk together flour, baking soda, salt, egg, lemon zest, and buttermilk until smooth.

Heat griddle over moderate heat until hot, then brush with oil.

Working in batches and using a ¼ cup measure filled halfway, pour batter onto griddle.

Cook, turning over once, until golden, about 2 minutes per side.

Peel the bananas and slice horizontally.

Sprinkle bananas with granulated sugar and place them in a non-stick baking pan.

Place bananas in broiler oven at 380°F until sugar slowly caramelizes. Remove. Let cool down and serve.

Stack 3 pancakes on top of each other.
Sprinkle confectioner's sugar.

Garnish with caramelized bananas and ½ strawberry on top.

Serves 4

Chef Ben Brown

Executive Chef | Courtesy of The Lodge at Pebble Beach
Pebble Beach, California

CHOCOLATE CHIP PANCAKES

Ingredients:

1¼ cups flour
1 tablespoon sugar
¼ teaspoon cinnamon
1 tablespoon baking powder
¼ teaspoon salt
2 eggs
1 cup milk
4 tablespoons melted butter
¾ teaspoon vanilla extract
1 cup chocolate chips (bitter or dark chocolate is best)

Preparation:

Combine flour, sugar, cinnamon, baking powder, and salt in a large bowl.

In a separate bowl, mix together eggs, milk, butter, and vanilla.

Beat the wet ingredients with the dry mixture until smooth.

Fold in chocolate chips.

Heat pan or griddle. Scoop the batter into the pan.

Hint: Use an ice cream scoop to get the right portion of batter on the grill, about 2½ ounces total for each pancake.

Flip the pancake when the top begins to bubble. Fry for 1 minute. Remove from pan and repeat until batter is gone.

Serve right from the griddle with unsalted butter and maple syrup.

"This recipe has been used for my children since they started eating solid food. We have always used an ice cream scoop for the batter so that the kids can be involved, and it is perfect for them to scoop without guessing on the amount."

Serves 4 – 6

Chef Justin Fields

Executive Sous Chef | Courtesy of The Ritz-Carlton, Denver

JOYCE'S CHOCOLATE CHIP PANCAKES

Ingredients:

4 tablespoons unsalted butter
1 cup milk (whole, 2 percent fat, or 1 percent fat)
1¼ cups flour
1 tablespoon sugar
4 tablespoons baking powder
¾ teaspoon salt
2 eggs
6 ounces semisweet chocolate chips (or less to taste)
butter, for cooking

Preparation:

In a small saucepan, combine the butter and milk.
Place over low heat just until warm and the butter is melted. Let it cool slightly.

In a bowl, combine the flour, sugar, baking powder, and salt. Mix well.

In a large bowl, whisk the eggs with a fork. Whisk in the milk mixture.

Add the dry ingredients and mix just until barely blended.

Heat a griddle or large skillet over medium heat.

Add about 1 teaspoon of butter and melt until bubbly.

Ladle 3 tablespoons of batter for each pancake onto the hot surface
and cook until bubbles begin to form on the edge of the bottom half.

Add the chocolate chips to the top of the pancakes.
This step is important to ensure that the chips keep a slight bite.

Cook for ten seconds and then turn and cook until golden brown on the other side,
about 30 seconds more. Repeat until all the batter is used up.

"This is what my Mom used to make for me as a kid ... it is fantastic!"

Serves 4 – 6

Chef Wendy Brodie

Executive Chef | The Art of Food: As seen on PBS
Carmel, California

FRUIT PANCAKES

Ingredients:

2 cups buttermilk pancake mix
2 teaspoons sugar
¼ teaspoon cinnamon
1 pinch nutmeg
¾ cup buttermilk
¾ cup orange-pineapple juice
½ teaspoon vanilla
1 large apple, coarsely grated including skin (no seeds)
1 banana, cut in ½ inch cubes
1 cup blueberries (thawed, if using frozen berries)
1 cup raspberries (thawed, if using frozen berries)
½ cup strawberries, cut in quarters (optional)
vegetable oil and/or butter, for frying

Preparation:

In a large bowl, blend pancake mix,
sugar, cinnamon, and nutmeg.

In a separate bowl, mix buttermilk, orange-pineapple juice, and vanilla.

Add the liquid mix to the dry mix and blend thoroughly.

Add grated apple, then banana; carefully fold in berries.

Note: Be careful not to break up the berries; this will discolor the batter.

The batter will look as though it is all fruit, coated with batter.

continued ...

Chef Wendy Brodie
FRUIT PANCAKES

For Crunchy Pancakes:

Heat a skillet to medium-low.

Melt butter or vegetable oil in a frying pan,
enough to cover the bottom of the pan.

Spoon a heaping ¼ cup of batter into the pan. When batter begins to bubble on top, flip over, making sure there is enough oil or butter for the other side to fry.

Note: If you are using frozen berries, the center of the pancakes take longer to cook, so place them into a 300°F preheated oven for 5 minutes to continue the cooking process without darkening them further, or turn the heat down on the skillet and flip the cakes a couple of times until done.

For Lighter Pancakes:

Spray a skillet with vegetable oil and heat over medium heat.
Spoon ¼ cup of batter into the skillet.

When bubbles appear on the batter, turn the cakes over and cook until desired color is achieved.

"Serve with your favorite heated maple syrup. I like good old-fashioned maple syrup. Also, sour cream or plain yogurt with honey is delicious. This pancake recipe was a family tradition on Sunday mornings with the Brodies. It was modified from a recipe that mother made with buckwheat flour, grated apple, raisins, and nuts. My brother and I didn't like the buckwheat taste. We had some buttermilk pancake mix, my dad's orange-pineapple juice, leftover berries, and bananas in the house. We also added grated apple to the batter and used sour cream and plain yogurt for our pancake topping. This was so delicious that it became the family favorite. When Bob and I got married we gave our favorite recipes to our guests and this recipe was one of them."

Makes 6 – 8 pancakes

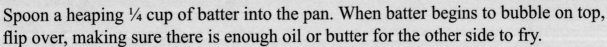

Chef Michael Chiarello

Bottega Restaurant | Napa Valley | California

HUCKLEBERRY PANCAKES

Ingredients:

1 large egg at room temperature
1¼ cups all-purpose flour
1¼ cups buttermilk
1 teaspoon sugar
1 teaspoon baking powder
½ teaspoon baking soda
½ teaspoon salt
huckleberry preserves
2 tablespoons melted sweet butter, for cooking

Preparation:

Heat griddle slowly while mixing batter.

To test, sprinkle with drops of water.
If bubbles "skitter around," heat is just right.

Wipe griddle with a little butter. Beat egg.
Measure flour and level, then sift it.

Whisk egg with buttermilk, then stir in the dry ingredients to a smooth batter.

Slowly pour batter onto griddle to desired pancake size.

Keep an eye on how the pancakes settle so as to determine
where to make the next one — be sure they don't touch.

When pancakes are puffed and full of bubbles, turn them and cook the other side.

Keep pancakes hot by placing them between folds
of warm towels in a warm oven. Don't stack them!

Serve hot and smother them with huckleberry preserves.

Serves 4 – 6

Chef John Zaner

Executive Chef | Courtesy of The Ritz-Carlton, Kapalua

KAPALUA PANCAKE BATTER RECIPE

Ingredients:

2 eggs
½ cup vegetable oil
½ cup sugar
2 teaspoons vanilla extract
2½ cups whole milk
2 cups all-purpose flour
2 tablespoons baking powder
1 tablespoon salt

Preparation:

Whip together eggs, oil, sugar, and vanilla.

Add 1 cup whole milk to mixture.

Add dry ingredients.

Mix until smooth.

Scrape, then add remaining milk. Mix.

Pour batter onto pre-heated skillet.

Add in any additional ingredients that you like,
for example, macadamia nuts, chocolate chips, or blueberries.

When batter starts to bubble, flip pancake over
and cook until lightly golden.

Serve warm.

Serves 4

Chef Cat Cora

"First and Only Female Iron Chef Cat Cora"

LEMON—PECAN PANCAKES

Ingredients:

1 ½ cups multi-grain/whole grain pancake mix
1 teaspoon raw sugar
1 lemon, zested
1¼ cups low fat milk, warmed slightly
1 large egg, beaten
2 tablespoons unsalted butter, melted
1 teaspoon vanilla extract
½ cup pecans, very finely chopped
maple syrup
fresh berries
powdered sugar

Preparation:

Preheat griddle pan or large sauté pan over medium heat.

In a large bowl, mix the pancake mix with sugar and lemon zest.

In a separate bowl, mix together the low fat milk, egg, butter, and vanilla.

Make a well in the center of the flour mixture.
Pour in the milk mixture and the chopped pecans.

Whisk just until well combined. Butter sauté pan or use cooking spray.

Spoon by ¼ cupfuls onto the griddle; be careful to not let edges touch.

Cook until the tops begin to bubble and just turn golden, about 3 minutes.
Flip pancake and cook for 1 – 2 minutes more, until light golden brown.

Transfer to plate and repeat with remaining batter until all pancakes are finished.

Serve hot, with maple syrup, fresh berries, and powdered sugar, if desired.

Serves 4

Executive Chef Don McPherson
Chef Andrew Trotter

Courtesy of Tehama Golf Club | Carmel, California

MEYER LEMON PANCAKES

Ingredients:

1 cup crème fraîche (reserve 1 tablespoon, for garnish)
2 tablespoons melted butter
1 large egg
½ cup freshly squeezed Meyer lemon juice
   (reserve 1 teaspoon, for garnish)
1 cup sifted all-purpose flour
2 tablespoons sugar
1 tablespoon zested Meyer lemon
powdered sugar, for garnish

Preparation:

In a large mixing bowl, combine crème fraîche, melted butter, egg, and lemon juice.

Whisk until thoroughly combined.

Add flour and sugar. Mix just until combined. Do not over mix.

Add lemon zest and stir gently until evenly distributed through the batter.

Heat a cast iron griddle to medium heat.
Melt some butter on griddle to keep from sticking.

Use a large tablespoon.
Dollop batter to create silver dollar sized pancakes.

Cook until bubbles pop up, about 3 – 4 minutes.
Flip and cook until golden brown.

Garnish with a drizzle of lemon juice, crème fraîche, and powdered sugar.

Serves 4 – 6

Chef Craig von Foerster

Executive Chef | Sierra Mar Restaurant, The Post Ranch Inn
Big Sur, California

PEANUT BUTTER & JELLY PANCAKES

Dry Ingredients:

1 cup flour
1 cup cake flour
¼ cup whole wheat flour
3 tablespoons sugar
2 teaspoons baking powder
1 teaspoon baking soda
¼ teaspoon salt
¼ teaspoon cinnamon

Wet Ingredients:

2 whole eggs
2 cups buttermilk
1 teaspoon vanilla extract
2 ounces melted butter
⅓ cup chunky peanut butter

Garnish:

⅓ cup jelly or jam, of choice

Preparation:

Sift all dry ingredients together.

Whisk all wet ingredients together.

Whisk wet ingredients into dry ingredients.

Lightly swirl ¼ cup of garnish jam or jelly into the batter.

Cook pancakes.

Note: Be careful not to burn the jam.

Serve with remaining jam or jelly.

"I think the first indication of my becoming a chef was how particular I was about style and amounts in regards to my Peanut Butter and Jelly Sandwiches."

Serves 4 – 6

Chef Marty Paradise

Culinary & Wine Educator | Santa Rosa, California

PARADISE PUMPKIN PIE PANCAKES

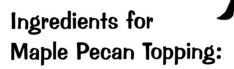

Ingredients for Batter:

¾ cups milk
2 tablespoons of pumpkin puree
1 egg
2 tablespoons vegetable oil OR for low fat use:
1 tablespoon vegetable oil & l tablespoon applesauce
1 teaspoon vanilla
1 cup all-purpose flour
2 tablespoons brown sugar
1 teaspoon ground nutmeg
1 teaspoon ground pumpkin spice
1 teaspoon ground cinnamon
1 teaspoon baking powder
½ teaspoon baking soda
½ teaspoon salt

Ingredients for Maple Pecan Topping:

1 cup maple syrup
1 tablespoon butter
¼ cup of chopped pecans
whipping cream, for serving

Preparation:

Mix all wet ingredients: milk, pumpkin, egg, oil, and vanilla. In a separate bowl, combine all the dry ingredients: flour, brown sugar, nutmeg, pumpkin spice, cinnamon, baking powder, baking soda, and salt. Stir into the pumpkin mixture.

Heat lightly oiled griddle or frying pan over medium-high heat.
Pour the batter onto the griddle using approximately ¼ cup for each pancake.

Brown on both sides and serve hot.

Heat syrup and butter together. Remove from heat. Throw in the pecans.
Spoon over pancakes. Top with whipping cream.

"Make sure to have lots of whipping cream to top it off! Besides, what is pumpkin pie without whipped cream? We make this family favorite the day after Thanksgiving, but with the great health benefits from pumpkins, try them more often."

Makes 10 – 12 pancakes

Chef Bert Cutino

CEC, AAC, HBOT, HOF | Co-Founder/COO, The Sardine Factory Restaurant
Monterey, California

RICOTTA CHEESE & CANDIED FRUIT PANCAKES

Ingredients:

1½ cups all-purpose flour
   (stir or sift flour before measuring)
2½ teaspoons baking powder
2 tablespoons cinnamon
2 tablespoons sugar
½ teaspoon salt
1 egg, slightly beaten
1½ cups cream or half & half
2 tablespoons butter, melted
1 cup ricotta cheese
¼ cup chopped candied fruit (optional)

Preparation:

Sift together flour, baking powder, cinnamon, sugar, and salt.

In a separate bowl, combine egg and cream.

Add to flour mixture.

Stir until smooth.

Blend in butter and ricotta cheese.

Add candied fruit, if desired.

Cook on hot, greased griddle.

Use about ¼ cup of batter for each pancake.

Cook until brown on one side and around the edge.

Turn and brown the other side.

Serves 4

Chef Michael Schmidt

Director of Operations for Stacks Restaurants, California
2007 Las Vegas Top 100 "Chef of the Year" | 2008 China Grill "Chef of the Year" Western Region
Executive Chef China Grill Las Vegas, Nevada

SWEET PANCAKE BATTER RECIPE

Ingredients:

1¼ ounces evaporated milk
2½ ounces water
6 large eggs, whipped
1 cup heavy cream
4 ounces butter
4 ounces margarine
4 cups flour
¾ cup sugar
¼ cup plus 2 tablespoons baking soda

Preparation:

Pre-heat skillet to medium heat.

Whip together the evaporated milk, water, eggs, and heavy cream.
Keep separate.
Melt the butter and margarine. Keep separate.

Mix the dry ingredients: flour, sugar, and baking soda. Keep separate.

Add melted butter mixture to the whipped ingredients.
Slowly add the dry ingredients into the wet ingredients.

Blend for 2 minutes until everything is incorporated and the batter is smooth.

Pour ¼ cup batter in pre-heated, oiled skillet.
Lightly brown over medium heat.
Add any desired additional ingredients, like blueberries, at this time.
Flip pancake after batter bubbles.

Cook time is typically 2 – 3 minutes on each side.

*"We like to add a tablespoon of wheat germ to each pancake once it is in the pan.
These are sweet, rich, and have been a family favorite for three generations."*

Serves 8

Chef Roy Yamaguchi

Master Chef | James Beard Award Winner

JAPANESE STYLE PANCAKE

Ingredients:

1 cup okonomiyaki flour blend
⅔ cup water
2 eggs
4 cups cabbage, thinly sliced
2 green onions, sliced
¼ cup tenkasu (tempura bits)
6 slices bacon, chopped and cooked

Preparation:

Use a large bowl.

Mix the okonomiyaki flour blend and water.

Mix thoroughly to form a smooth batter.

Add the eggs, cabbage, green onions, and tenkasu.

Heat a non-stick pan over medium heat.

Pour the pancake mixture into the pan to form a pancake.

Place the bacon on top of the batter.

Cook for about 3 – 4 minutes.

Flip over.

Serves 4

Chef Adrian Hoffman

Vice President and Culinary Director | Lark Creek Restaurant Group
San Francisco, California

POTATO LATKES

Ingredients:

3 russet potatoes
1 small onion
½ teaspoon sea salt
pinch white pepper
4 ounces sour cream
4 egg yolks
⅔ cup freeze dried bread crumbs or crushed matzoh
2 ounces clarified butter, for frying
1 fresh apple, shaved
watercress, for garnish

Preparation:

The night before: Bake the russet potatoes in a 350ºF oven for one hour.
Puncture the potatoes with a knife; when the knife comes out easily,
the potatoes are ready.

Store the potatoes in the refrigerator overnight.

Peel the skin from the potatoes.
Grate coarsely on a box grater.

In the same bowl, grate the onion, then add salt, pepper,
sour cream, egg yolks, and bread crumbs.

Mix gently until all ingredients are incorporated.

Heat the clarified butter over medium heat in a non-stick pan.

Take 2 ounces of the mixture and pat into the shape of a patty.

Brown well on one side, flip over and brown again.

Serve hot with shaved fresh apple and watercress.

Serves 2 - 4 or serves 4 as a side dish

Chef Peter Merriman

Executive Chef | Owner Merriman's Restaurants | Hawaii

POTATO PANCAKES

Ingredients:

⅔ cup of diced onion, uncooked
3 cups of peeled and diced red potato, uncooked
2 eggs
1 tablespoon bacon grease
¼ teaspoon cayenne pepper
2 teaspoons salt
1 teaspoon malt vinegar
⅔ cup sour cream, plus ⅓ cup, for garnish
applesauce, for garnish

Preparation:

In a blender, place onions and potato and pulse until smooth.

Hint: If your blender is smaller, split into 2 or 3 batches.

Add eggs, bacon grease, cayenne pepper, salt, malt vinegar, and ⅔ cup sour cream.

Heat a non-stick sauté pan to medium-high.

Ladle batter into pan forming 4-inch pancakes.

When bubbles form and then burst, flip, then cook for 1 minute longer.

"Sit down and eat 'em up immediately. Great with sour cream garnish or applesauce."

Serves 4

Chef Colin Moody

Executive Chef | Monterey Peninsula 2007 Chef of the Year
Courtesy of Monterey Peninsula Country Club | Pebble Beach, California

SMOKED CHEDDAR & BACON POTATO PANCAKES

Ingredients:

½ pound potatoes, peeled and cut
¼ cup buttermilk
1 egg
2 tablespoons all-purpose flour
2 slices smoked bacon, cooked and chopped
¼ cup smoked cheddar, shredded
2 tablespoons chives, finely sliced
¼ teaspoon salt
¼ teaspoon pepper
2 tablespoons unsalted butter
sour cream, for garnish

Preparation:

In medium saucepan, add potatoes to boiling water.
Return to a boil; reduce heat to medium.
Cook, covered, about 12 minutes or until tender. Drain.

Use electric hand mixer or potato masher. Mash potatoes until smooth.

Beat in buttermilk and egg until blended.

Stir in flour, bacon, cheese, chives, salt, and pepper.

In large nonstick skillet, heat butter over medium heat.

For each pancake, drop 2 tablespoons potato mixture into pan.

Cook 2 – 3 minutes per side, or until golden brown, turning once.
Drain on paper towels.

*"Enjoy with sour cream. Serve at lunchtime with a salad
or serve as a side dish for dinner."*

Serves 4 – 6

Quickly's Glossary

Anticipation: looking forward to

Approached: came closer

Bedazzled: fascinated

Brochures: pamphlets, booklets

Camp: a place to go for fun and friendship

Descendant: relative

Dimmed: lost its luster

Distributed: gave out

Fortuitous: occurring by lucky chance

Fount: source

Gathered: came together

Historian: a student or writer of history

Knowledge: something learned

Implements: tools, utensils

Magical: giving a feeling of enchantment

Percolated: trickled or filtered

Reinforced: strengthened

Sauntered: walked leisurely

Savory: flavorful without sweetness

Scrumptious: delicious

Sundry: different

Slyly: craftily, secretively

Traditions: customs that are handed down over the years

Trusty: dependable

Visions: vivid pictures

QUICKLY HAPPILY ACKNOWLEDGES:

His Family:
The Abelmanns & The Cohens

His Contributing Friends:
Ron Abelmann, David & Julia, Danielle and Rochelle Abelmann,
Michael & Wendy, Charlotte and Holden Abelmann, Nancy Abelmann,
Carole Alter, Fiona Applebaum, Mike Bowhay, Bob Bussinger, Ashley R. Campbell,
Doug Chang, Mollie & Art and Jeffrey Cohen, Marcella Costa, Michael Dellar,
Stephen Donahue, Robin Duffy, Tom Feltz, Denise Foderaro, Norma Galehouse,
Andrew Gardner, Daryl Griffith, Carol Horner, Jo-Ann Seitman Jacobson,
Karin Johnson, James Kellogg, Herb Kronish, Danielle Kuck, Lien Ho-Lin,
Sharon & John and Kean Matthams, Nanci Markey, Jenny Ochtera,
Dawn Rodriguez, Nina Rodriguez, Daniel Seward,
Barbara Shaw, Nancy Shea, Joelle Steefel,
Deniese Steelman, Dan Tibbitts, and Hal Valentine.

His Editors Extraordinaire:
Kathryn & Ben Perry for your expertise.
Nita Lelyveld for your magic touch.

His Friends:
The Great Chefs

Author:

Miriam Kronish teaches at Cambridge College in Massachusetts. Over the past decades she has taught at Lesley University in the Creative Arts in Learning Master's Degree Program. She is a retired principal from the Needham (MA) Public Schools. Her interests are music, educational pursuits, cooking, theater, reading, and especially writing. She is a National Distinguished Principal and an Honored Principal in the State of Massachusetts. She is a Past President of the Needham Rotary Club. She lives in Massachusetts with her husband.

Author:

Jeryl Abelmann is a retired elementary school teacher. She is the recipient of Teacher of the Year for the San Ramon Valley Unified School District in California. A member of The Carmel Bach Festival Board of Directors, the California Writers Club, and the Screen Actors Guild, she loves the movies, theater, writing, and traveling. She has two sons and four adorable grandchildren. She and her husband live in Northern California.

Illustrator:

Chason Matthams is the 2011 "Children's Books Winner" for his illustrations for *Quickly: The Magic Spatula* from the Hollywood Book Festival. He is a graduate of the Fine Arts Department of New York University. His artistic works include illustration, painting, and portraiture. He is currently pursuing his MFA in studio art at NYU, where he is also an adjunct professor teaching painting and drawing. He lives in New York City and has shown his artwork in galleries from New York to San Francisco.